The Adventures of Little Skippy

BETH BACH

ReadersMagnet, LLC

With dark clouds spanning the sky, and trees swaying back and forth from the strong force of the blowing winds, heavy flakes of snow were beginning to fall. The air temperature was dropping quickly. All the animals of the forest knew when a storm was coming, and tonight was that night. They had to find shelter quickly!

The bears of course didn't have to worry because they were already in their dens. They found their homes in late summer and early fall when they started to feel sleepy. They would dig into the ground to make a large hole then cover or hide under heavy piles of leaves and brush, or they might find a large opening inside the trunk of a decaying tree. There they would curl up and hibernate all winter long. When spring arrived and the snow started to melt they awakened, stretched, and left their home to find berries, nuts, fish, and other sweet foods to fill their empty stomachs. They didn't even know when snowstorms came during the winter. They were sound asleep.

Coyotes, bobcats, wolves, and weasels didn't sleep like the black bears did, they continued to roam the forest looking for food. Being carnivores they ate meat, not berries and nuts. But tonight they settled down waiting until the storm passed.

Deer, elk, antelope, big horn sheep and moose grew a thick coat of fur to keep them warm, but they knew not to venture too far from their homes. They had to stay far away from the predators that were looking for their next meal, but tonight they worried more about the coming storm.

Bobcat

Coyote

Ermine Weasel in winter with its white fur coat

Herd of elk

Having lived through many terrible winter storms, Skippy's mother knew how important it was to keep Skippy safe. She raised two female fawns the previous year and was quite proud they survived the cold harsh winter. But this winter was different.

Skippy was born two months later than the other mule deer fawns. He still had white spots that baby fawns are born with to help camouflage or hide them in the thick bushes when their mother was away. These spots disappear in three to four months after birth usually by late autumn when the fawns are stronger and able to follow their mother into the deep forest.

Skippy's mother knew he would have trouble walking through the heavy snow that covered the ground. She worried that if he had to run to get away from a coyote, he might not be able to get away fast enough. Finding food might also be a problem. She could easily eat the bark from the trees, but she worried that little Skippy might be too small to reach it.

As the winds pushed hard against her body, she brought Skippy closer to her side while they rested under a large pine tree. The tree's branches gave some protection from the falling snow and strong blowing wind. But with the large flakes of snow coming down so fast, it was harder for her to see. The snow was beginning to cover her face and eyes.

Without the moon and stars shining through the sky to provide light in the forest she had difficulty seeing anything moving nearby. She had to rely on her keen sense of smell and hearing to remain aware of any dangers. Her instincts told her to stay alert during this terrible storm, so she could protect Skippy.

Little Skippy and his mother

Little Skippy and his mother

The night seemed to pass slowly. She looked down at him as he appeared to be sleeping peacefully while she tried her best to keep him warm. She loved him dearly. She was a good mother.

By morning, the storm had passed. The sun was shining brightly casting colorful sparkles of light on the soft white snow. Skippy's mother began to rouse or awaken him. She was hungry and had to find food.

"Skippy, did you sleep well during that awful storm last night?" she asked nudging him with her nose.

Glancing up to see her face looking down at him Skippy said, "Good morning, Mama. I heard a lot of strange sounds. What were they?"

"It was the howling of the strong winds and blowing snow. I hope it didn't frighten you too much," she replied.

"You kept me warm, Mama. I knew not to be afraid because you were by my side," he calmly answered.

"Oh that is good, Skippy. I didn't want you to be frightened. I must leave you for a little while to find some food to eat in the forest. While I am away, you must lie very still so no other animals of the forest can hear or see you. Remain quiet in this patch of brush until I return."

"Okay, Mama. I will do as you ask, I will try to sleep some more," Skippy answered.

"I will return soon my son," as she slowly wandered into the forest while continuing to listen for wolves and coyotes.

Skippy trying to sleep in the winter storm

Skippy looking about

Skippy not liking snow in his face and eyes

Skippy listening for movement of nearby creatures

Because Skippy was so young, he didn't have a scent or smell coming from his little body. This was nature's way of protecting baby fawns. Coyotes and wolves had a keen or excellent sense of smell for finding their prey, but not for baby fawns.

To keep the evil creatures or predators from finding him, he kept still and silent.

After a few hours, Skippy's mother returned and cautiously approached him not wanting to frighten him as she came nearer.

"Skippy are you awake?" she quietly asked.

Opening his eyes, Skippy saw his mother standing beside him. As he stood up, she offered him her warm rich milk for nourishment knowing he was quite hungry.

As the weeks passed, and Skippy became stronger, his mother felt comfortable leading him to different areas of the mountain where he could eat shrubs, twigs, and grasses from the forest ground and drink water from the flowing stream in the valley below.

Skippy

Skippy and his mother

"Follow me closely Skippy, I will take you to a nice place where there is much food to eat," she instructed as she walked on a trail through the woods.

Skippy saw lots of pine trees and aspen trees and little creatures moving about as he and his mother walked along the path.

"Who are these little guys?" he asked.

"They are birds, squirrels, chipmunks, and other creatures that live here in the forest with us, Skippy," his mother answered.

She continued, "They will not harm or hurt you. They are friendly. But you must remember there are other creatures in the forest that will try to hurt you; you must stay far away from them."

Skippy's mother leading little Skippy down a trail

Skippy saying "hello"

Chipmunk

Squirrel

Downy Woodpecker

Clark's Nutcracker

Black-billed Magpie

"How will I know which are nice and which are not nice?" he asked.

"I will let you know my son," she assured him.

He saw large dark blue birds flying from tree branch to tree branch. These birds he learned were called Steller's jays. An even larger black and white bird was flying from the tree branches to the ground below getting nuts and seeds to eat. This bird was called a magpie.

"Hello birds, my name is Skippy!" he shouted.

"Hello Skippy. What a fine day! The snow is melting!" answered the chickadees, the nuthatches, and the woodpeckers.

Steller's Jay

Red Crossbill Finch

Dark-eyed Junco

"You make pretty sounds," Skippy told them.

"We love to sing Skippy! We like to make beautiful music for the rest of the forest creatures to enjoy," they explained.

"I sure like it. I wish I could sing," Skippy said sadly.

"Skippy, you have other talents. You can jump high and run fast. Someday you will become king of the forest," they smiled.

Skippy wasn't too sure if they were right about him becoming a king. He saw many other deer in the forest who were much bigger.

Somedays they made him feel sad. When he tried to walk over to the other fawns playing in the forest, they looked at him and laughed.

"Go away Skippy, you are too little to play with us," they told him.

Skippy didn't understand why they didn't like him. He just wanted to be their friend.

"Mama, the other fawns won't let me play with them," Skippy cried.

"Why do you say that Skippy?" his mother asked.

"When I walk up to them, they laugh at me and tell me to go away," as tears started to fall from his eyes.

"Skippy, I wish they would be nice to you. I will talk to their mothers. But I want you to always remember something. One day you will become bigger and stronger than these other fawns. They will forget that they once made you cry and instead look at you with pride because they know you will help protect them from the evils of the forest.

Skippy

Skippy

    With the coming of spring, Skippy found new food to eat as the flowers popped up through the thawing warm ground. Sometimes he got so excited about these tasty treats, that he wandered too far from his mother's sight. When he looked up and didn't see her standing nearby, suddenly Skippy became frightened.

    "Mama, where are you?" Skippy called.

    Soon he heard deer hooves walking up the forest ridge. He listened closely and decided to walk in that direction. He was so happy to see his mother grazing or eating the tall grasses.

    "Oh Mama, I was so scared! I thought I was lost!" Skippy cried running towards her.

    "Skippy, it can happen in this dense or thick forest. You must stay close by my side and follow me," as she calmly touched his forehead with hers.

    One summer day, Skippy saw a big deer with a rack of antlers on his head.

    "Why does that deer look so different from us, Mama?" Skippy asked.

    "He has antlers, Skippy. Only male mule deer have them. One day you will have those too. He grows new antlers every spring after they fall off in the winter," she told him.

    "They fall off! Why?" he wanted to know.

    She continued, "Every year, he will grow a new set of antlers, sometimes larger than the year before. The deer with the largest set of antlers will be king of his part of the forest. Other bucks will try to fight him for it, but he will let them know it belongs to him. You will see this someday."

"Do they get hurt when they fight?" Skippy asked with a worried look.

Mule deer buck with rack of antlers

Mule deer bucks with antlers locking together

His mother answered, "Sometimes that can happen, but usually they lock their antlers together for just a short time until one of the bucks pulls away. They learn who is the stronger of the two very soon. The weaker buck has to go away to find a different place to claim for his own."

"Okay," Skippy said slowly not sure if he really understood what his mother was telling him.

One summer day, Skippy found a friend. He was so happy!

"Hi, my name is Skippy. What's yours?" Skippy wondered as he looked down at the nearby furry animal eating tall grass.

Looking up at Skippy, the creature stopped chewing long enough to say, "Hello, my name is Hopper, and I am a rabbit".

Skippy sees a rabbit for the first time

Skippy curious about the rabbit

Skippy eating beside the rabbit

"Nice to meet you, Hopper. How did you get that name?" Skippy asked.

Laughing, Hopper said, "Watch me go from this patch of grass over to this other patch of grass."

"Now do you see how I got my name?" he grinned.

"Oh yes! You hop around. That is a good name for you," Skippy smiled.

"I like this tall grass too. Do you mind if I stay here and eat some?" Skippy asked.

"Of course not, there is enough for both of us," Hopper said.

Where do you live Hopper?" Skippy wanted to know.

"Not too far from here. I have several homes. Since coyotes and bobcats travel near here, I don't want them to know where I live. So I move from one home to the other from time to time.

Today, I live in a big hole in the ground near that pine tree over there," pointing to the large tree several yards away.

"Does your mama live there too?" Skippy asked.

Hopper answered, "No, I live alone. I am too big now to live with her. She told me it was okay for me to find a place of my own last year."

"Oh, that is nice. But don't you get lonesome sometimes?"

"No, I see mama and my brothers and sisters too. They don't live too far away. We say hello when we hop past each other," Hopper replied.

"That is so nice. Well, I sure enjoyed talking to you. I guess I had better go now. My mother told me to stay close to her so I wouldn't get lost."

"That is good advice Skippy. You have a good mama. Bye now," as Hopper hopped away to find a new stock of tasty grass.

Skippy liked his life in these mountains. Several times he heard the howling from the coyotes in the distance, but his mother made sure they never came close enough to harm him. When she sensed they were near, she instructed Skippy to pronk or jump as quickly as possible through the woods to get away from them.

One fine day, Skippy heard a shout from the top of a nearby tree.

"Hello down there!" came the sound from a dark black furry creature.

Black bear cub climbing up a tree

Black bear cub standing near a pine tree

Baby black bear sitting

Baby black bear running

Baby black bear with its mother

Baby black bear with its mother

As Skippy looked up into the top of the tree he saw two dark brown eyes staring back at him.

"Who are you? My name is Skippy and I live in this forest with my mama. She is right over there. "

"Yes, I see her. You look just like her only smaller," the furry creature laughed.

"How did you get up there; aren't you afraid you might fall? You haven't told me your name," Skippy asked.

"Well, I don't think I have a name, but I love to eat wild strawberries, so I think I will call myself Strawberry. Do you like that name?" she asked.

"Oh, that is a lovely name. Now you better get down from up there before you fall," Skippy said with a worried look on his face.

"I won't fall because I have long sharp claws to hold on tightly to the tree bark. All bears have claws. I love to climb trees because I can see far distances from up here," she replied.

"I don't have claws," he said while scratching his right ear with his back hoof.

"Skippy, every creature is different here in the forest. As you make new friends you will notice that, but we still like to stop and say hello as we pass by," Strawberry replied.

"It makes me happy to know who lives in this big forest where I live too," Skippy said.

"You will make lots of new friends Skippy," answered Strawberry.

"Oh, that is good! I must go now; my mama is calling me. Goodbye Strawberry, I will see you again soon," Skippy told her.

"Goodbye Skippy," as Strawberry slowly started to climb down from the tree.

As the weeks passed, Skippy's legs could now move swiftly through the brush under the forest trees. He became more curious about his surroundings as he became more confident.

Skippy's mother knew, being a male deer, he would not stay by her side all the time as her female fawns did in past years. But after teaching him how to survive and protect himself, she was no longer worried.

Skippy began to quietly follow behind the bucks as they grazed in the meadows below the mountains. They seemed to accept him knowing that he would grow up to be like them and develop antlers like theirs. They also knew they might one day have to fight him.

While Skippy watched, he saw two large bucks slowly walk towards each other. They were deciding who was the stronger. They would run toward each other and bow their heads until their antlers would lock together. They would push and pull and push and pull until one of them became tired. The weaker buck would wander away to find another place in the forest to claim as his own just as his mother said they would.

Skippy saw animals much taller than he was and asking his mother who they were, she said, "There are herds of elk in this forest, but you will usually see them in the meadows grazing on the grasses. There are other animals of the forest that are much bigger even that the elk."

"I think I know that now Mama," Skippy answered proudly.

"You do?" she asked.

"Yes, I saw an animal with hooves just like we have but this new friend was much taller and had dark fur and a big nose, I remember," Skippy said, thinking back to the day when he and his mother had gone down into the meadow to drink from the pond.

It was a beautiful sunny afternoon and suddenly after he took a big drink of that cold water, he saw a very tall brown animal standing several yards away in the deeper area of the pond. It had just lifted its head up out of the water while chewing on something.

"What are you eating over there?" Skippy yelled.

"Nutritious grasses that grow on the floor of the pond. This is how I get my daily vitamins," answered the smart long-legged animal.

As he slowly started to wade through the water and walk closer to Skippy he said, "Hi, my name is Buddy. I used to be scared to get too close to the edge of the pond. But my mother taught me not to be afraid and slowly I would follow her into the water and find this delicious food down at the bottom. So now I come here every spring and summer to make sure I get the proper food to eat for my body to get strong."

"Oh my! That is good. My name is Skippy and I only come down here to the edge of the pond to get a drink of water. If you don't mind my asking, why do you have such a large nose?" Skippy wanted to know.

"Well, I am not really sure, except I had this nose when I was born. Some other animals used to laugh at me, but I didn't mind because my sisters also have this big nose and of course my mother and father do too. I just get used to the laughing. I am an incredibly good swimmer while some other animals are not," he answered proudly.

Continuing he said, "I close my nostrils, these large openings at the end of my nose, when I dunk my head down below the surface of the water to pull the grasses up from the bottom. Then of course I raise my head back up and take a deep breath," he explained.

"That is so interesting. I like learning how each of us is different," Skippy stated.

As he thought about this, Buddy replied, "That we are indeed! But this is what makes our lives interesting and these differences we can share. It helps us to know each other better."

"You are so wise, Buddy! I hope I will be as smart as you someday," Skippy sighed as he took another sip of water.

"Oh, you will be, Skippy. You are starting already by asking a lot of questions. That is how you learn." Buddy smiled as he was leaving.

When Skippy told his mother, who was now sitting down on the forest ground resting, this story of meeting that animal at the pond she said, "That was a moose. They usually hide in the bushes or briars and they love to go into the ponds to eat the grasses that grow deep under the water as he explained to you."

When summer moved into fall, Skippy's mother gently told him, "Skippy, I have something to tell you. Since I have taught you everything I know for you to survive in the forest, you no longer need me to guide you. You are now ready to go off on your own. I am so proud of you and I know you will do well being by yourself."

Baby moose calves hiding under aspen trees

Baby moose calves with their mother

Moose calf running through the forest

Adult male bull moose starting a growth of new antlers

Adult male bull moose

Female moose cows eating shrubs

Male bull moose eating shrubs

"I can go anywhere I want to go?" he asked.

"Yes, Skippy, you have grown up. You don't need me to be with me anymore," she said, smiling.

Skippy loved his mother and felt sad to leave her, but he also knew she was right and that it was time for him to go out on his own while continuing to explore the forest hillsides.

Skippy had now grown two spikes at the top of his forehead. He was still too young to fight older stronger bucks, but he knew one day that his time would come.

After they said goodbye to each other he slowly walked up the mountain ridge until he could no longer see her. He had tears in his eyes, but he wanted to appear strong, so he quickly wiped them away. He never forgot the things she taught him, and he knew one day he would see her again. If another buck approached him to fight, he believed he could win. He was becoming that strong proud buck that his mother said he would become!

One year old Skippy

Year old Skippy

Four-year-old Skippy

FUN FACTS

Ermine (weasel family) – they have long bodies and short legs; the tip of their tail is black. In summer they have a dark brown coat of fur, but in winter that coat turns white giving the weasel the ermine's name. They are carnivores which means they eat rodents, small birds, and fish. They can climb trees and swim through the water. They move in a zigzag motion, bouncing 20 inches from the ground and can travel nine miles a night in search of food.

Moose – the largest member of the deer family, are herbivores which means they eat birch tree bark, aspen twigs, and other shrubs. The male is called a bull while the baby moose is called a calf. The male's antlers can spread 6 feet from end to end. A dangling hairy dewlap called a bell hangs down from their neck. They have a pendulous muzzle (nose and mouth) and they measure 7 feet tall at the shoulder.

Magpies – are omnivores meaning they eat berries, grains, and bugs. They are considered to be one of the smartest animals in the world.

Black bear – when in winter hibernation, they survive off their body fat. They reabsorb their urine. They have an excellent sense of smell, 100 times better than humans. They can live to be 18 to 23 years old.

Rabbits – their range of vision spans nearly 360 degrees allowing them to see what is behind them, to the side of them and above without turning their heads. They chew 120 times a minute. They spend a lot of time grooming themselves.